THE CHRISTMAS GNOME

Written by: Ashleigh Corbin

Book Dedication

This little tale is for Miss Nellie Marie. Her pure joy and genuine love for life inspires me everyday to live better.

1

'Tis the season of joy and waiting for gifts unknown,
'Tis the season for festivities and for the arrival of...

The Christmas Gnome!

The Christmas Gnome arrives in the
month of December,
He will stick around for awhile and is
pretty even tempered.
With a twinkle in his eye and a heart
so bright,
He spreads joy and wonder on snowy
days and every starry night.

When your gnome comes home, give it a name and make it unique, Something that fits its personality: merry, spunky and sleek. For your gnome has come this Holiday to stay, Bringing warmth and happiness, every single day.

9

He finds cozy nooks, where he will try to hide,
Looking for a new spot to discover on every night of yuletide.
As you wake with giggles and your eyes all aglow,
Make sure to search for your gnome friend, both high and low.

He will join tea parties and games
of tag by day,
And as twilight approaches, he will
sneak away,
To bring smiles and laughter, oh so sweet,
To the children he cherishes, a memory
for them to keep.

13

Then when Christmas day comes, your
Christmas Gnome will be so happy.
He will unwrap
gifts and take
family pics, and
even dress up all
fancy.
With a heart full
of kindness and
pockets of cheer,

The Christmas Gnome will make
the season so dear.

15

As the holiday season comes to an end,
The Christmas Gnome will say farewell
to every new friend.
But The Christmas Gnome will leave
each year with more than a smile,
He will leave you with memories that
will last in your heart, for a while.

The End

Meet the Family

Meet the Corbin family, the creative minds behind *The Christmas Gnome*. At the helm is Ashleigh Corbin, a mom with a heart full of holiday spirit. Her inspiration for this heartwarming tale came from her own daughter's wonder and excitement during the Christmas season.

The Corbin family's passion for making the holiday season special shines through in every page of this enchanting story, making *The Christmas Gnome* a beloved addition to countless families' Christmas traditions.

Tradition of The Christmas Gnome

Introducing *The Christmas Gnome*, a delightful tradition designed to bring the magic of the holiday season to life for kids and families in a fun and stress-free way. As a mom, I have meticulously avoided a certain holiday tradition that has swept across the nation. Please know, if you are a part of bringing happy elf's into your home each year- continue to do so. That is your tradition and I applaud your tenacity and creativity. However, if you find yourself being begged by your children again this year to be a part of that tradition and find it daunting...The Christmas Gnome is for you!

I realized the reason my daughter wanted to be apart of something over the month of December was to simply enjoy the magic of Christmas. Thus, the concept of The Christmas Gnome came to be. A gnome that arrives in your home. He hides at night (no shenanigans) and when your child finds him hiding the next day, they have a new friend to play with and share in all the Christmas festivities.

It keeps it simple.
It keeps it fun.
It keeps it imaginative for your kids.

You can pick up your own gnome from a local store or make one from some stuffing and fabric. Just remember to hide him somewhere new every night...and if you forget that, it's ok. He is only around for the month of December.

Ashleigh Corbin

Made in the USA
Monee, IL
01 December 2024

71939970R00017